DISNEY

# HORSETAIL Hollow ★ ★

# STUPENDOUSLY SAMSON

4

# STUPENDOUSLY SAMSON

By Kiki Thorpe

Illustrated by Laura Catrinella

DISNEP · HYPERION

Los Angeles    New York

First Hardcover Edition, March 2023
First Paperback Edition, March 2023
10 9 8 7 6 5 4 3 2 1
FAC-058958-23027
Printed in the United States of America
This book is set in Goudy Old Style Std/Monotype; Laughing Gull/Atlantic Fonts
Designed by Joann Hill
Illustrated by Laura Catrinella

Library of Congress Control Number: 2022948678
Hardcover ISBN 978-1-368-09422-1
Paperback ISBN 978-1-368-09424-5
Reinforced binding for hardcover edition
Visit www.DisneyBooks.com

For Aubrey and Harper

Maddie Phillips and her little sister, Evie, stood side by side on the farmhouse porch. Together, they watched as an old red pickup truck drove up the lane to Horsetail Hollow.

Maddie's stomach fluttered with excitement. She'd been waiting for this moment for days, and now it was here!

The truck rolled to a stop in front of their house. The door opened, and a girl in jeans and cowboy boots hopped out. Her grin lit up her whole face. "Hi, you guys!"

"Macy!" the sisters cried in unison. They ran over and wrapped her in a three-way hug.

Macy's grandmother Rosalyn stepped down from the truck. Her tan face crinkled in a smile. "It's nice to see you girls together again," she said.

"Thank you for letting Macy stay over," Maddie said, breaking out of the hug.

"I had to!" Rosalyn said with a laugh. "All I've heard since her last visit was, 'When can I see Maddie and Evie again? When can I go back to Horsetail Hollow?' If Macy couldn't come, I'd never have heard the end of it," she added with a wink.

Rosalyn was the Phillipses' closest neighbor, but Macy lived in the next town over. The girls had met one day when Macy came to her grandmother's farm for a visit. Right from the start, they'd seemed destined to be friends. Macy was nine years old, just like Maddie, and just like Maddie, she loved horses.

Macy also liked adventures, which was a good thing . . . because Horsetail Hollow had a magical secret.

On the farm, there was a wishing well. Ever since Maddie and Evie had thrown in a penny and made a wish together, they'd had one enchanted adventure after another. And now Macy was in on the secret, too.

"So, girls, any special plans tonight?" Rosalyn

3

asked, her dark eyes twinkling. Maddie always had the feeling that Rosalyn knew something she wasn't telling. But she could never be sure.

"Just games, maybe a movie. You know, the usual sleepover stuff," Maddie said.

"Sounds wonderful. Come here, Macy, and give your gram a kiss good-bye." Rosalyn opened her arms, and Macy stepped into them.

"Bye, Gram," she said as Roslyn planted a kiss on her forehead.

"I'll pick you up in the morning. Have fun, girls!" Rosalyn climbed back in the truck and started it up. With a wave, she pulled away.

"Come on, let's go to the barn," Maddie said.

Horsetail Hollow's old barn sat a short distance from the house. Horses had once lived there, but those days had long since passed. The barn's red paint was now faded and peeling. There were gaps in the sides, and holes in the roof. The barn was where

Maddie did all her best daydreaming. And it was where she and Evie had made their discovery.

The wishing well was hidden in a clump of trees and tall grass not far from the barn. Maddie and Evie had spotted it one day while playing in the hayloft. That day, they both wished on the same penny. Evie had wished to meet a fairy-tale princess. Maddie had wished for a horse. When a fairy-tale horse named Maximus showed up on the farm, they realized their wishes had come true—but they'd gotten mixed up!

Maximus had come to them straight from "The Story of Rapunzel" in Evie's storybook. Ever since then, fairy-tale horses kept turning up in Horsetail Hollow. Each time, it was up to Maddie and Evie to get the horses back to their fairy-tale homes. Without them, there couldn't be a happily-ever-after!

Even though the wishing well hadn't granted their wishes the way they'd imagined, their wishes had still come true. Evie had met three real fairy-tale princesses. And Maddie had gotten to ride three magnificent horses.

The last horse to visit was Philippe from "The Story of Beauty and the Beast." Macy had helped him save his story. So now she was in on Horsetail Hollow's secret, too.

"Tell me everything!" Macy said now as the three girls sat down in the hay. "Have you seen Philippe? Or Belle? What happened since the last time I was here?"

Maddie and Evie glanced at each other.

"Nothing," Evie said.

Macy's face fell. "Nothing?"

"Nope," said Maddie. "It's been weirdly unmagical around here."

"Did you make any new wishes?" Macy asked.

"We tried," Evie said. "But they didn't come true."

"We wished to see Maximus," Maddie explained. "Angus and Philippe, too. We wished we could visit them without changing their stories, or they could visit us. But nothing happened."

"Maddie thinks maybe the magic got used up," Evie said.

"I wonder," Macy said thoughtfully. "Or maybe the wishing well just doesn't know how to grant your wish."

Maddie hadn't thought of that. "Why would a wishing well grant some wishes and not others?" she asked.

Macy shrugged. "Beats me." She leaned back on her hands. "It's too bad, though. I was really hoping we could see Philippe again."

Maddie sighed. "Me too."

Once, Maddie's greatest wish had been to have her own horse. But even though they weren't hers to keep, the fairy-tale horses had been the most wonderful horses she'd ever met. She longed to see them again.

"At least I can visit your grandma's horses," she said to Macy. "And I was thinking of asking Mom and Dad if I could go back to Sunny Stables. Hey . . . maybe you could go, too!" Sunny Stables was the camp where Maddie and Macy had both learned to ride.

"Didn't you hear?" Macy said, looking surprised. "Sunny Stables is closing."

"What?" Maddie sat straight up. "*Why?*"

"The owners are retiring," Macy said. "This is the last summer they'll run the camp."

Maddie felt stunned. Sunny Stables held a special place in her heart. It was where she'd fallen in love with horses.

But that wasn't the only thing that made it special. Most horse-riding lessons were expensive. But Sunny Stables gave lots of kids the chance to ride, not just the ones who could afford to pay. If it hadn't been for Sunny Stables, Maddie wasn't sure she'd ever have discovered how amazing horses could be.

She thought of all the kids who would never learn to love horses. And the horses who would miss out on those kids' love.

"I just can't believe it," she said.

"Yeah, it's sad," Macy agreed.

It *was* sad. But Maddie wasn't going to let the news ruin her first-ever sleepover with Macy.

She jumped to her feet and dusted off her hands. "Who's up for a game of horseshoes?"

## CHAPTER
# TWO

"Okay, I've got one," Macy said.

The girls were sprawled on the floor in Maddie's room. It was past bedtime, but they were having too much fun to go to sleep.

Macy took a handful of popcorn from the bowl between them. "Would you rather live in a castle or a tree house?" she asked.

"That's easy!" said Evie. "Castle!"

"No surprise there," Maddie said, eyeing Evie's pink princess nightgown. She munched some popcorn, considering the question. "It depends. Does the tree house have a bathroom?"

Macy nodded. "It's a luxury tree house."

"Then tree house, definitely," Maddie said.

"Me too," said Macy. "I'd pick the tree house. But only if my mom and dad could live with me. And Gram, too, of course."

"Same. I'd want a tree house big enough for my whole family. Even Evie," Maddie said, giving her sister a playful nudge. "My turn. Would you rather be able to fly or turn invisible?"

"Easy!" Evie said again. She picked up one of Maddie's stuffed horses and tossed it in the air. "Fly!"

"Ooh, that's a tough one," Macy said. "Fly, I guess. How about you, Maddie?"

"Being invisible. So I'd always win at hide-and-seek." Maddie covered her mouth as she yawned.

"Are you tired?" Macy asked. "We can go to sleep if you want."

"No way!" Maddie hopped up. She wasn't going to waste their sleepover sleeping! She picked up the popcorn bowl. "Who wants more snacks?"

"I do!" Macy and Evie said in unison.

"I'll be right back," Maddie said. Holding the empty bowl, she hurried downstairs.

There was a light on in the kitchen. Her parents were sitting at the table, talking. Maddie was about to go in. But something in their voices stopped her.

"You mean, sell our land?" Mom was saying.

Maddie paused outside the doorway, listening.

"It's a good offer, Ann," Dad replied.

"But all the land west of the barn? That's nearly half the farm," Mom said.

*West of the barn?* Maddie thought. *But . . . that's where the wishing well is!*

"This farm has always been bigger than we can manage on our own. We aren't using those acres for anything," Dad said. "They'll be worth more to someone else."

Maddie shrank back into the shadows. There was a heavy feeling in the pit of her stomach.

If Mom and Dad sold the land, what would happen to the wishing well? Maddie hated to think. The new owners might put up a fence. Or they might seal up the well without even a crack to throw a coin through.

Maddie had an even worse thought. What if they tore the well down to make room for something else? How would she ever see her fairy-tale friends again?

She crept back upstairs, still holding the empty

bowl. When she walked into her room, Macy and Evie were laughing. But they stopped when they saw Maddie's face.

"What's wrong, Maddie?" Macy asked.

Maddie hesitated. She didn't want to spoil the sleepover with more bad news.

"Nothing." Maddie smiled weakly. "I guess I'm just tired after all."

Later that night, Maddie lay awake, tossing and turning in bed. No matter how she tried, she couldn't fall asleep. Her mind was racing.

She couldn't let Mom and Dad get rid of the wishing well. There had to be some way to stop it.

Maddie sat up. She could make a wish. A wish to save the well!

Maddie got out of bed and took a penny from her

coin jar. Macy lay asleep in her sleeping bag. Her braids fanned out on the pillow like rays of the sun. Maddie thought about waking her, then decided against it.

The house was dark and quiet as Maddie tiptoed downstairs. She opened the back door and slipped outside.

It was late at night, but Maddie wasn't afraid. She knew the path well, and a full moon lit the way. She hurried around the pond and down past the barn, until she came to a little grove of trees.

The old stone well peeked up from the tall grass, greeting her like a friend.

Maddie squeezed her penny. She tried to think of exactly the right wish.

She could wish that the land wouldn't be sold. But what if her parents needed the money? Ever since they'd moved to the farm, it seemed like they were always worried about bills.

Maybe she could wish for a fortune. If they were rich, they wouldn't need to sell their land.

But sometimes when the wishing well granted a wish, it took something away from somewhere else. Whose fortune might she end up stealing?

No, Maddie decided. That wish wouldn't do.

She could wish that nothing would ever happen to the well. That seemed safe.

But the more Maddie thought about it, the more that seemed like the worst wish of all. What if that meant nothing *ever happened* to the well again? No more wishes, no more magic. A wish like that was the same as sealing up the well for good.

Maddie sighed. "I just wish I knew what to do," she said.

She dropped the coin into the well. Then she hurried back to the house.

She slipped under the covers and soon fell into a restless sleep.

18

CHAPTER
THREE

Maddie was dreaming.

In her dream, she was back at Sunny Stables
Riding Camp, riding in the ring. Her horse was a
white gelding with a glossy black mane. Maddie had
never seen this horse before, but in the dream they
were old friends.

Round and round the ring they galloped. Each
time the horse's hooves struck the ground, tiny
sparks appeared. They left a shimmering trail of

magic that seemed to spread in circles, wider and wider. Maddie had never been so happy—

"Maddie!"

A voice punctured her sleep. Maddie burrowed into her pillow. She tried to hold on to the wonderful dream.

"Maddie, wake up!"

Maddie opened her eyes. She wasn't riding a magical horse. She was lying in her own bed. Macy was leaning over her. The full moon shone brightly in the window behind her, silhouetting her head.

"There's a horse outside," Macy whispered.

Suddenly Maddie was wide-awake. She sat up. "What horse?"

Macy shook her head. "I don't know. I've never seen it before."

Maddie got up and went to the window. A large ghostly shape was standing in the field.

It *was* a horse! In the moonlight, the horse's

white coat almost seemed to glow. Maddie wondered if she was still dreaming.

Macy joined her at the window. Together they looked out at the mysterious visitor.

The horse stood quietly, hardly moving. He looked like he was waiting for something.

"How did you know he was there?" Maddie asked.

"The moon was so bright, I couldn't sleep. I went to the window to close your curtains, and I saw him! Do you think the wishing well sent him?" Macy whispered.

"Maybe," Maddie said, remembering her wish from earlier that night. "Come on. Let's see what he wants."

The girls tiptoed downstairs, and slipped out the back door. Dew dampened the cuffs of their pants as they ran across the grass.

As they came closer, Maddie saw that though the horse's coat was white, his mane and tail were

black. He wore an old-fashioned saddle with a chest plate and fancy breeching. Maddie felt a flash of recognition. She'd seen this horse before!

"He's just like the horse in my dream!" she said with a gasp.

Macy looked at her. "What dream?"

"Tonight I dreamed I was riding a horse just like this one," Maddie explained. The wonderful feeling of the dream washed over her again.

When the horse saw Maddie, he raised his head. His ears went forward, and his eyes brightened. He gave a friendly nicker.

"I think he knows you, too." Macy shivered. "Ooh! I just got a chill down my spine. This is like a fairy tale!"

"But what's he doing here?" Maddie wondered.

"Don't you see?" Macy said, gripping her arm. "You've met before . . . once upon a dream. Maybe *this* is the horse you were always meant to have. The wishing well made your dream come true at last!"

Maddie's heart did a somersault. Could it be? Had the wishing well finally granted her wish?

As if he could hear her thoughts, the horse suddenly tucked one foreleg and bowed to her. The gesture was so gallant and old-fashioned, Maddie could imagine him saying, *Hail, gentle maiden. I am at your service.*

"I think he wants you to go for a ride," Macy said.

The horse chuffed affirmatively.

"Okay. But you have to come with me," Maddie said to Macy.

The horse was big, but he bowed again, lowering himself so Maddie and Macy could climb onto his back.

When they were in the saddle, Macy clasped her arms around Maddie's waist, and they set out.

They rode in silence. The only sound was the quiet clop of the horse's hooves. There were no sparks or magical hoofprints. But Maddie still felt as if she were in a dream. The fat moon hung above them, round and shiny as a new coin. It frosted the trees with silver and made the pond glimmer. In its light, the tired old farm seemed to take on a new splendor.

But maybe it was more than the moonlight. For as they rode, Maddie became aware of a sound, like music that was too faint to hear. The air hummed, and she could have sworn she glimpsed will-o'-the wisps among the weeds. For a brief moment, all of Horsetail Hollow seemed magical.

It was over too soon. Moments later, or so it seemed, they were back at the farmhouse. Maddie climbed down from the horse's back. The farm looked ordinary again. But when she and Macy locked eyes, Maddie knew she'd sensed the same thing.

Maddie put the horse in the paddock. "Thank you for the ride," she said, petting him. "See you in the morning, I hope."

A band of pale blue showed at the edge of the sky as Maddie and Macy slipped into Maddie's room. Maddie was so tired she was asleep as soon as her head touched the pillow. But she went to sleep smiling.

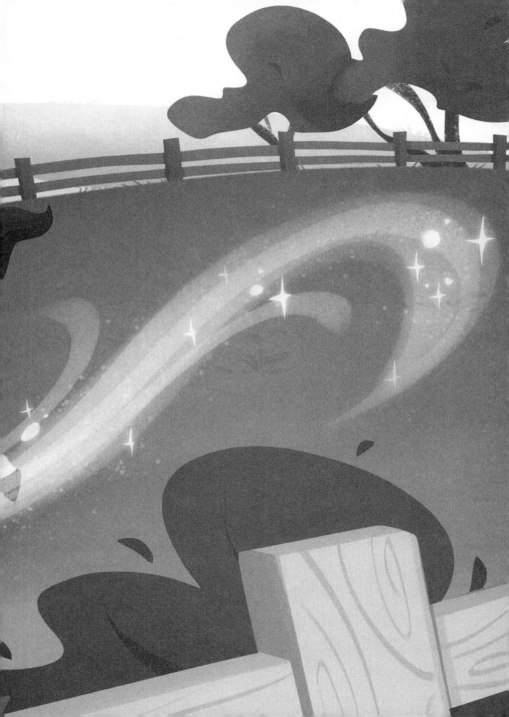

CHAPTER

FOUR

"Rise and shine!" Dad exclaimed.

Maddie peeled her heavy eyes open. Sunlight flooded her bedroom.

Her dad was standing in the doorway.

"Time to get up. It's a beautiful day!" he said.

A lump moved inside Macy's sleeping bag. Macy poked her head out, blinking in the bright light. She looked as tired as Maddie felt.

"You girls look exhausted," Dad remarked.

"Let me guess. You stayed up all night talking, didn't you?"

*All night?* Maddie thought, still sleepy. Then she remembered. *The horse! The moonlight ride!*

Macy sucked in her breath, and Maddie knew she was thinking the same thing.

"When you're ready, come down for breakfast. I made pancakes," Dad said.

When he was gone, Maddie and Macy jumped up and raced to the window.

The paddock was empty.

"Where is he?" Maddie pushed the window wide open and leaned out as far as she dared. She searched around the pond, the garden, and all the fields. The white horse was nowhere to be seen.

"It wasn't a dream. Was it?" she asked Macy.

Macy shook her head. "I was there, too."

"But where did he go?" Maddie asked.

"I don't know." Macy put her arm around Maddie's shoulders. "My mom always says we think better after a good breakfast. Let's eat. Then we'll figure out what to do."

Downstairs, two plates piled with pancakes sat on the kitchen table. Dad was at the stove, pouring more batter into the pan.

"Dig in," he told the girls. "Evie, Mom, and I already ate."

Maddie and Macy had just taken their first bites when the back door banged open. Evie rushed in, out of breath. She was wearing her princess pajamas and a pair of rubber boots. A lopsided plastic crown clung to her curls, as if it was holding on for dear life.

"Guys, I found something," she said when she saw Maddie and Macy. "Come see!"

"In a minute, Evie. We're eating," Maddie said.

Evie hovered by her elbow. "Can you eat faster?"

Maddie poured more syrup on her pancakes. "What did you find?" she asked without much

interest. Knowing Evie, it was probably a ladybug or a sparkly rock.

"I'll give you a clue," Evie said. "It's black and white. It likes carrots." She leaned close to Maddie and whispered in her ear. "And it's in the barn *right now.*"

"Oh," Maddie said. Then it dawned on her. "*Oh!*"

"Hmm," Dad said. "What's black and white and likes carrots? A caterpillar? No, let's see . . . a magpie?"

Maddie hopped up from the table. She signaled Macy. *We've got to go!*

Macy's eyes widened. She got up, too, gulping down the rest of her orange juice. "Thanks for breakfast, Mr. Phillips. It was delicious."

"A skunk?" Dad said, still puzzling over Evie's riddle. "Please tell me it's not a skunk, Evie . . . Evie?"

The back door slammed. They were already gone.

"Where did you find the horse?" Maddie asked Evie as they raced to the barn.

"I saw him outside when I got up this morning," Evie explained breathlessly. "You and Macy wouldn't wake up. So I put him in here."

They stepped into the barn. There he was—the white horse with the glossy black mane.

When the horse saw Maddie and Macy his ears pricked up. He bowed his head and gave a courtly nicker, as if to say, *Ah! The two maidens from last night. I've been awaiting your return.*

"I got him into the barn all by myself," Evie said proudly. "I got a carrot, and I waved it in front of his nose. And he followed me! I even gave him some hay." She pointed to the feed bin. "Did I do good?"

"You did great, Evie." Maddie couldn't tear her eyes from the horse. He was even more beautiful in the daylight, if that was possible.

Maddie's heart beat a rhythm that seemed to say, *At last. At last. At last.*

"What are you going to call him?" Macy asked.

"I'm not sure," Maddie said. A horse this magnificent deserved a grand name. "Maybe Atlas or Neptune or . . . I know! Galaxy!"

"You can't name him Galaxy," Evie said matter-of-factly.

"Why not?" asked Maddie.

"Because he already has a name," Evie said. "He's Samson, Prince Phillip's horse!"

"Prince Phillip?" Maddie's happiness deflated like a popped balloon. "Who's Prince Phillip?"

"I'll show you." Evie ran out of the barn.

She returned a moment later with her big book of fairy tales. Evie had read it so many times that its cover was worn. She knew every story by heart.

She opened the book and turned to "The Story of Sleeping Beauty."

Evie pointed to a picture of a young man. He was standing alone in the woods. "That's Prince Phillip. He's Sleeping Beauty's true love."

Samson looked over her shoulder and whinnied happily. *Ah, my dear friend, Phillip! Never was there a more loyal companion.*

Maddie studied the picture. Prince Phillip wore a dashing red cape and a matching feathered hat. He looked like just the sort of person who would ride a big, strong, regal horse.

A horse just like Samson.

"I don't understand," Maddie said, rubbing her head. "It doesn't make sense. Why would the wishing well send another fairy-tale horse? How is that supposed to help save the well?"

"What do you mean *save the well?*" Macy asked.

Maddie told them what she'd heard about her parents selling part of the farm.

"That's awful!" Macy said with a gasp. "Why didn't you tell us?"

"I didn't want to ruin our sleepover," Maddie explained. "While you were sleeping, I made a wish to figure out what I should do. But I still don't have a clue. . . . Evie, are you even listening?"

Evie was staring at the picture in her book. "That's weird," she said, frowning.

"What?" asked Maddie.

"Usually, Princess Aurora and Prince Phillip are together in this picture," Evie told her.

The girls looked at one another, eyebrows raised. "You don't think . . . ?" Macy started to say.

A loud yawn interrupted her. It had come from the hayloft.

"Goodness," said an unfamiliar voice. "What a dream!"

CHAPTER

FIVE

Maddie, Macy, and Evie looked toward the hayloft. Maddie put a finger to her lips. Then they quietly climbed the ladder. They peeked around a stack of hay bales.

A teenage girl was sitting in the hay, stretching as if she'd just woken up.

The girl's dress was wrinkled, and bits of hay were stuck in her hair. But her locks were as golden as a ray of sunlight. And her lips, stretched wide in a yawn, were as red as a rose.

Maddie didn't need to know any story by heart to guess who she was. Somehow, Sleeping Beauty had landed in their barn.

When she spied the girls, Sleeping Beauty's blue eyes opened wide. "Oh, my goodness!" she exclaimed. "I didn't realize anyone else was here." She had a high, sweet voice that reminded Maddie of little birds singing.

"Princess Aurora?" Evie whispered in awe.

The princess frowned. "Please don't call me that. My name is Briar Rose. You can call me Rose, if you like. I hope you don't mind that I slept in your barn," she added quickly. "You see, I was just so very tired last night. And the hay looked so comfortable."

Maddie blinked. "Um, Rose . . . would you excuse us for a second?"

The girls ducked back behind the stack of hay bales.

"What's *she* doing here?" Maddie whispered, giving Evie an accusing look.

Evie's eyes widened. "How should I know? *I* didn't wish for her."

Maddie put her hands on her hips. "Well, someone did! And it wasn't me."

"It wasn't me either!" Evie insisted.

Macy held up her hands. "Don't look at me! Sleeping Beauty isn't even my favorite fairy tale."

"Oh boy," Maddie said. "This is bad! We almost messed up three different fairy tales just by wishing for a horse. Think what's going to happen when Sleeping Beauty's *princess* goes missing!"

"Maddie's right," Macy said. "We have to send her back."

"No, thank you," Briar Rose said loudly from the other side of the hay bales.

The girls went silent. They peeked around at the princess.

"What did you say?" Macy asked.

"I said, 'No, thank you,'" Briar Rose repeated, politely but firmly. "I can hear you whispering over there. And I don't want to go back."

"You don't?" Maddie asked, surprised. "Why not?"

"It's just . . ." Briar Rose paused. Her lip began to tremble. "Well, you see . . . oh, everything is awful!" she cried. Then she burst into tears.

The girls kneeled beside her in the hay. Evie squeezed her hand. Macy patted her back.

"What happened?" Maddie asked gently.

"Today was my sixteenth birthday," Briar Rose said, dabbing at her eyes. "I thought it would be just like all my other birthdays. First we have cake. Then I sing and dance with some bunnies and squirrels."

"That sounds like a nice birthday," Evie said.

"It is." Briar Rose sniffled. "But this year, I hadn't even blown out the candles when my aunts told me the most *horrible* news. . . ." She choked back a sob.

"What news?" Maddie asked.

"I'm a *princess!*" Briar Rose wailed.

"You don't *want* to be a princess?" Evie goggled at her like she couldn't imagine such a thing.

"Why should I?" Briar Rose asked, wiping her nose on her sleeve. "My life is perfect! I spend my days in the woods, doing whatever I like. I know every animal in the forest, and they're all my friends.

Now they want me to go live in some stuffy old castle and attend boring banquets and wear itchy dresses and . . . *shoes*." Briar Rose shuddered. "Worst of all, they say I have to marry some awful prince I've never even met. If you were me, you'd run away, too!"

The girls gasped.

"You ran away?" Macy asked.

"I did." Briar Rose lifted her chin. Her eyes flashed defiantly. "When my aunts sent me to my room to change into my royal gown, I slipped out the window."

"Gosh," said Evie.

The princess sighed. "I suppose they'll be worried," she added. "I feel sorry about that. But what else could I do?"

"But how did you end up *here* in Horsetail Hollow?" Maddie asked.

"It was the strangest thing," Briar Rose replied.

"Earlier today, I met a boy. I meet lots of animals in the woods. But a boy? He was handsome and charming. It felt like a dream!"

As Briar Rose spoke, a change came over her. Her eyes shone, her cheeks glowed, and a smile crept over her face.

"It sounds silly, I know," she said, blushing slightly. "After all, we'd just met. But I felt like I knew him. Isn't that strange?"

"Not really," Maddie said. That was exactly how she'd felt when she saw Samson.

"That doesn't explain how you got to Horsetail Hollow," Macy pointed out.

"I'm getting to that," Briar Rose said. "Later that night, when I climbed out my window, I saw that boy's horse."

From below, there came a loud whinny. Samson was listening.

Briar Rose went to the edge of the hayloft. She

looked down into the barn. "That's him! Hello, you!" she called.

Samson nodded his head. *And a good day to you, fair maiden!* he nickered.

"I thought surely that nice boy would be back soon, so I went over to wait for him," Briar Rose explained. "But then I heard my aunts' voices. They'd discovered I was missing! I had to leave quickly. And by chance, we were standing next to a well. . . ."

Maddie suddenly guessed what was coming next. "So you made a wish," she said.

"How did you know?" Briar Rose asked in surprise. "Yes, I wished I was somewhere far away. At once, a terrible storm came up. The wind blew, and the world started to spin. The next thing I knew, I was here."

So Samson was here because of Briar Rose's wish, Maddie thought. But that still didn't explain why they'd ended up in Horsetail Hollow.

And Maddie had made her own wish, a wish that had nothing to do with Briar Rose's. Unless . . .

Maddie gasped. "The wishing wells are connected!"

Everyone turned to her. "What do you mean?" Macy asked.

Maddie grabbed Evie's book of fairy tales. She quickly turned the pages. "That's why our wishes keep bringing horses from fairy tales. Because our wishing well is a *fairy-tale well!*"

Maddie triumphantly held up the book. It was a picture of Briar Rose's cottage in the woods. A well stood in the background—a well that looked exactly like theirs.

But the friends never had time to ponder their discovery. At that moment, three figures rushed into the barn. They wore dresses of red, blue, and green, with matching cloaks and pointed caps.

Despite their strange clothes, their faces were ordinary. They might have been anyone's aunts, except for one thing. They all had wings.

"Rose!" exclaimed the tall fairy in red. "Thank goodness we found you!"

"Aunt Flora!" Briar Rose exclaimed. "Aunt Fauna! Aunt Merryweather! What are you doing here?"

"Oh, Rose!" The green fairy's eyes filled with tears of relief. "We've been worried sick!"

"We thought that old witch Maleficent had gotten you!" added the stout fairy in blue.

"I'm sorry I worried you, Aunt Fauna and Merryweather," Briar Rose replied, casting her gaze downward. She really did look sorry. "But how did you find me?"

"Merryweather spied your footprints, and we followed them to the well. When they stopped there, we guessed what had happened," Fauna explained.

Flora shook her head. "I always said a wishing well would lead to trouble. But *Merryweather* wanted it," she added with a scowl.

The blue fairy folded her arms. "What good is a well if it doesn't grant wishes?" she huffed.

"Anyway, all that's behind us," Flora said, turning back to Briar Rose. "Now let's get you fixed up, and we'll be on our way."

Maddie sighed with relief. Thank goodness the fairies had arrived. They would fix everything!

Flora took a wand from her cloak. She flicked it once, and the hay flew out of Briar Rose's hair. With another flick, the wrinkles vanished from her dress.

"Much better," Flora said. "Now, we must be off to the castle. We have a birthday party to attend!"

Briar Rose took a deep breath. "I'm not going," she said.

"Of course, you are, dear. You're the guest of honor," said Fauna.

"I mean I'm not going back." Briar Rose's voice trembled, but she went on. "I don't want to be a princess."

"Nonsense, child," Flora replied. "Who doesn't want to be a princess?"

"Not everyone does, Flora dear. Some may prefer prancing barefoot through the forest. Why don't we discuss this over a nice cup of tea?" Fauna said.

She twirled her wand. A teapot and teacups appeared in midair. The pot filled the cups with steaming tea.

"Here we are," Fauna said, passing them around. "One lump or two, Rose, dear?"

"I don't want tea." Briar Rose was starting to look exasperated. "Did you hear what I said?"

"Yes, child. We heard." Flora sipped from her cup. "But we promised your father, King Stefan, we'd bring you home this evening, and he's expecting us. So we'll have to sort something out."

Flora set down her cup. She tapped her wand against her palm, thinking. "I know! We'll turn her into a flower!"

Samson's ears flicked forward. He snorted as if to say, *Surely, my ears deceive me. Did she say . . . a flower?*

"What a good idea! A flower can't run away," Fauna said enthusiastically. "She'll make a lovely tulip!"

"No, dear, a *Rose*," said Flora.

"Yes, of course," Fauna agreed with a sigh. "But I do so like tulips."

Maddie and Macy glanced at each other. A flower? What kind of plan was that?

"It won't work," Merryweather declared, much to Maddie's relief. But then the blue fairy added, "A flower can't have a birthday. And the party is already planned."

Samson nickered and shook his head, as if to say, *These three are not the sharpest nails in the horseshoe, are they?*

"We could turn her into a songbird," Fauna suggested. "They have birthdays, don't they?"

"But then she could fly away. And that's no different from running away," Merryweather pointed out.

Maddie glanced at Briar Rose. The princess was sitting on a hay bale with her chin in her hand. She wore a bored, unhappy expression. Maddie had the feeling she'd heard this sort of conversation before.

As the fairies went on discussing flowers and songbirds and birthdays, Evie picked up the book of fairy tales. She turned a page, and her eyes widened.

"Um, Miss Flora . . . ?" Evie said.

"Just a moment, dear," Flora said, pouring herself more tea. "What about a tortoise? They're much easier to catch."

Fauna clasped her hands in delight. "They're easy to catch *and* they have birthdays!"

"Miss Merryweather . . . ?" Evie tugged the fairy's sleeve.

"One second, child," the fairy said, waving her off. "We'll give her a beautiful blue shell!"

"No, pink!" said Flora.

"YOU GUYS!" Evie shouted, turning rather pink herself. *"What about Prince Phillip?"*

"She's right, you know," Fauna said. "We have to think of Phillip. Would he rather marry a blue tortoise or a pink one?"

With an impatient snort, Samson trotted to Evie's side. He nudged her with his nose as if to say, *Pray tell! What news do you have of my prince?*

"He's been captured by Maleficent!"

Evie held up the book. In the picture, Prince Phillip was sitting in a dark dungeon cell. His hands and feet were chained. "If *you're* all here, who's going to save *him*?" she asked.

Samson let out a horrified whinny.

"Oh, my stars!" exclaimed Flora.

"That's the boy I met in the woods!" cried Briar Rose. She put her hand to her forehead. "Oh dear. I told him where I lived!"

"Maleficent must have caught the poor boy at the cottage," Merryweather said.

Samson reared up and whinnied, as if to say, *I must go to him at once!*

"We'll help you!" said Flora. "Maleficent's castle is a fortress of evil. He'll need every bit of our magic to escape!"

The fairies and Samson turned to leave the barn. But they found the way blocked.

Mom and Dad stood in the doorway. From the looks on their faces, Maddie could tell they'd seen everything.

"Are those real . . . ?" Dad murmured.

"Fairies? Uh-huh," Mom replied, looking dazed.

"Are you two all right? You don't look well," Flora said, peering at their pale faces.

"That's our mom and dad," Evie informed her. "They're not used to magic."

"I see. Let me make them more comfortable." Flora raised her wand.

"Allow me," Fauna said, raising hers too.

"But it's my turn!" exclaimed Merryweather.

At the same moment, three streaks of magic shot from three different wands. They collided in the air over Mom and Dad.

At once, the grown-ups relaxed.

"I feel so sleepy," Dad said with a yawn.

"I just need to rest my eyes for a minute," Mom said as her eyelids drifted shut. Within a moment, they were fast asleep.

But the spells bounced off each other. They exploded outward, raining down magic . . .

over Flora,

over Fauna,

and over Merryweather.

One by one, the fairies' eyes closed. They slumped to the floor, snoring sweetly.

Maddie, Evie, Macy, Briar Rose, and Samson looked at one another.

"Oh boy," Maddie said. "I didn't see *that* coming."

"Wake up, Aunt Flora," Briar Rose said, shaking her. "Please! Wake up!"

Flora rolled over, snoring.

"Aunt Fauna! Aunt Merryweather! We need your help!" Briar Rose patted their hands and pinched their cheeks.

But the fairies slept on, smiling as if they were having the most pleasant dreams.

"It must be a really strong sleeping spell," Macy said.

"What will we do?" Briar Rose asked, wringing her hands. "Without their good magic, there's no hope of getting through Maleficent's castle. They said so themselves."

"I have an idea!" Evie leaned down. She took the wand from Flora's sleeping hand. "*We'll* be the good fairies!"

"Us?" Maddie asked.

"Yes! Genius, Evie." Macy picked up Fauna and Merryweather's wands. She handed one to Maddie. "It's perfect. There are three wands—one for each of us!"

Maddie held the wand between her fingertips as if it might explode. "But we don't know how to use them!"

"It can't be hard." Evie waved her wand experimentally. A stream of bubbles shot from the end.

"Eek! Evie, don't point that thing!" Maddie ducked as the bubbles went over her head.

"It's okay, Maddie. Good fairies can only do magic that brings joy and happiness. At least, that's what my book says." Evie waved her wand again. A fountain of whipped cream sprayed out the end. She squirted it into her mouth and giggled.

"I know what makes *me* happy." Macy waved her wand.

*Poof!* A plate of frosted cupcakes appeared. Macy took one and bit into it. "Mmm, chocolate!"

"Yes, please." Evie helped herself.

"Guys, be serious! How are bubbles and cupcakes going to help us in a fortress of evil?" Maddie asked.

"Don't underestimate cupcakes," Macy replied with her mouth full.

Samson nudged Maddie with his nose. He nickered gently. *Take heart, my friend,* he seemed to say. *It is not the sword but the knight who wins the battle.*

"You're right, Samson," Maddie said. They couldn't let Samson face Maleficent alone. If the good fairies' wands were all they had . . . well, they'd just have to do their best with them.

Besides, it *did* look fun.

Maddie gave her wand a practice wave. A thousand pennies rained out of the air and clattered to the floor. Maddie scooped up a few and put them in her pocket. Just in case.

"Okay. I'm ready," she said.

"Just one more thing," Macy said, aiming her wand at Evie.

Evie squeaked as a streak of green sparkles hit her. She turned to look over her shoulder. A tiny pair of wings had sprouted on her back.

Evie fluttered them and rose into the air. "Ooh! Look at me! I'm a real fairy!"

"Now do me!" Macy told her.

Evie fired a sparkling pink blast. A moment later,

both girls were flying around the room on their
new wings.

"This. Is. So. COOL!" Macy said.

They both turned to Maddie, raising their wands.

Maddie shook her head. Just watching them
made her stomach feel swoopy. "No, thanks. I'll stick
to riding," she said.

She got onto Samson's back. Briar Rose climbed
into the saddle behind her.

Samson reared up, pawing the air. *To the wishing well!*

When they were gathered around the well, Maddie and Briar Rose got off of Samson. Maddie pulled a penny from her pocket.

"Put out your hands," she said, holding the coin out on her palm. "We all need to wish together."

Evie and Macy placed their hands on Maddie's. Samson added his hoof. Briar Rose put out her hand, too.

Then she lowered it.

"Rose?" Maddie asked.

Briar Rose stepped backward. "I can't," she said.

"Are you scared of Maleficent?" Evie asked.

Briar Rose shook her head no. "As soon as I go back, I'll become Princess Aurora. I'll never get to be just plain old Rose again. I wish—" She glanced at the coin in Maddie's hand and sighed. "I just want things to stay the same."

Maddie didn't know what to say. Briar Rose was right. Once she returned to her fairy tale, she would be a princess for always.

But her story needed her. Without the princess, there could be no happy ending.

Maddie looked at the penny. Then she closed her hand and put it in her pocket.

"Maddie?" said Evie.

"What are you doing?" Macy asked.

"It's Briar Rose's story," Maddie said. "She should decide how it ends."

Briar Rose looked uncertain. "I want to help Phillip," she said. "But I love my life the way it is."

"Your wish is important," Maddie said. She thought for a moment. "But what if your wish could help lots of people? Not just Prince Phillip."

Briar Rose blinked. "What do you mean?"

"If you don't go back, your story ends," Maddie explained. "Maybe Samson and the three of us can rescue Prince Phillip without you. But Maleficent will still win. As long as she's around, the people in your kingdom will always live in fear."

"I could change that?" Briar Rose asked.

Maddie nodded. "If you break the curse." Then she added, "You don't have to be the kind of princess you think they want. You can be your own kind of princess."

Briar Rose looked down at her feet. No one said anything. They waited to see what she would do.

At last, Briar Rose raised her head. "Where's that penny?" she asked.

Maddie held it out with a grin.

Briar Rose placed the penny in her palm. Maddie, Evie, and Macy put their hands on hers. Samson added his hoof.

"On the count of three," Maddie said. "One . . . two . . . *three*."

In a swirl of red, green, and blue smoke, they were gone.

CHAPTER

# EIGHT

When the smoke cleared, they were standing on a bare mountaintop. Nothing grew, not a tree or a flower or a blade of grass. A steady drizzle fell from the dark clouds. The place had a feeling of misery and despair.

Maddie shivered. "Where are we?"

"The Forbidden Mountain," Evie replied in a whisper. "And there's Maleficent's castle."

Ahead, the ground fell away to jagged rocks

below. On the other side of the ravine, an enormous castle perched at the edge of a cliff. Its towers looked like arrows aimed at the sky. A narrow wooden bridge was the only way across.

"Look, the door is open," Macy said, pointing.

The castle's gateway yawned like an open mouth. A goblin holding a tall axe guarded the entrance.

Samson gave a low nicker. He pawed the ground with one hoof. Briar Rose nodded.

"Sorry," said Maddie. "I didn't catch that."

"He says now all we have to do is slip past the guard, find the dungeon, free Prince Phillip, and get out before Maleficent finds us," Briar Rose

explained. "Oh, and he also said, 'Be strong, my faithful companions. For a battle is won by a courageous heart.'"

"You got all that from a *nicker?*" said Macy.

Briar Rose shrugged. "I told you, all my friends are animals. But how are we going to get past that guard?"

"We could make him fall asleep, like the good fairies did to Mom and Dad," Evie suggested, eyeing her wand.

"We can't get close enough to cast a spell. He'll see us!" Macy said.

"Oh! That's it!" Maddie waved her wand.

At once, they disappeared.

"Where are you guys?" Evie squealed.

"Maddie? Samson? Briar Rose? Where did you go?" Maddie felt Macy's hand grope her face.

Samson whinnied. *Unhand my mane!*

"Everyone, stop freaking out! We're all here. At least, I think we are."

Maddie held up her hands. She couldn't see them. She clapped them together and felt them touch, but she looked right through them. It was a strange feeling.

"I made us invisible," she explained. "Now we can sneak past the guard."

"Good thinking!" Macy's voice said from somewhere to Maddie's left.

"Everyone hold on, so we don't get separated. And don't make a sound," Maddie warned.

Holding tightly to each other, they started toward the castle entrance. All seemed well until they reached the bridge. Suddenly, they heard:

*Clop-clop-clop.*

The sound echoed on the hollow wood.

"Samson!" Maddie hissed. "Your horseshoes!"

Samson froze. They watched in horror as the goblin guard raised his head. He looked around suspiciously.

"I've got this," Evie whispered. Maddie sensed

her flick her wand. Samson gave a soft snort of surprise.

He took another step. This time, his hooves were silent.

"Slippers," Evie explained.

With Samson tiptoeing in his slippers, they sneaked past the guard and through the castle gate.

Maddie had hoped they could sneak to the dungeon without being noticed. But as they stepped into the great hall, her blood ran cold.

The castle was crawling with hideous goblins!

Some had fangs, others had snouts or batlike ears. Some had hardly any face at all. They carried clubs and deadly looking spears.

Maddie felt Evie's small hand grip hers.

Samson nickered low, as if to say, *Steady hearts, my friends.*

"Remember, they can't see us," Briar Rose whispered.

"But there are so many of them," Maddie whispered back. "How will we get through?"

"We'll just have to stay close," Briar Rose said. "Is everyone ready?"

"Ready," Evie whispered.

*Ready,* Samson nickered.

"Ready," Maddie gulped.

They waited.

"Macy?" she whispered. *"Macy?"*

There was no reply.

Oh no! They'd lost Macy!

Just then, they heard a commotion on the other

side of the room. A group of goblins were fighting over something. They clawed and scratched at each other, trying to get at whatever it was.

As their shrieks echoed around the room, the crowd grew larger. More goblins piled in. They reminded Maddie of sharks feeding.

Suddenly, she heard Macy's voice right in her ear. "The path is clear! Let's go!"

"Where were you?" Maddie asked as they hurried past the frenzied mob.

"Creating a distraction," Macy explained.

At that moment, a goblin staggered away from the throng, holding a prize.

Maddie stared. "Are those . . . ?"

"Cupcakes," Macy said, and Maddie could hear the smile in her voice.

"Look, these stairs lead down!" Briar Rose whispered, and she rushed down the stairwell she found. They quickly followed after her.

Downstairs, they found the dungeon behind a heavy wooden door. Macy and Evie used their wands to pick the lock.

When they pushed the door open, Prince Phillip jumped to his feet. "Who's there?" he cried out.

Samson whinnied joyfully. *My prince! It is I, Samson!*

But Phillip continued to search the air blindly. "I hear my faithful horse. But I see no one. Have my eyes been cursed?"

Oops! They were still invisible!

"My bad." Maddie waved her wand, and they reappeared.

"Samson!" the prince cried, throwing his arms around the horse's neck. He looked at Briar Rose in astonishment. "And you're here, too! But how did this happen?"

"We'll fill you in later," Macy told him. "Right now, we have to get out of here."

Maddie, Evie, and Macy set to work undoing his chains with their wands. The prince kept looking at Briar Rose. He couldn't seem to tear his eyes away from her.

And, Maddie noticed, she was gazing at him, too.

"By the way," Prince Phillip said, "I don't think I got your name."

"I'm Rose. . . ." Briar Rose hesitated. Then she smiled. "But you can call me Princess Aurora."

"Got it!" Maddie exclaimed as the last chain fell free. "Come on, let's get out of here!"

But as they turned to the door, a wall of green fire blazed up, barring their way. A gaunt,

green-skinned fairy appeared amid the flames. She wore a black cloak and a horned headdress. Her purple eyes gleamed with malice.

Evie gasped. "Maleficent!"

"Fools!" Maleficent cried. "You dare to defy me, the Mistress of Evil?" She raised her scepter.

*We're in for it now,* Maddie thought. What would Maleficent do? Blast them away? Summon the goblins? Turn them all into toads?

Maleficent struck her scepter against the floor. In a flash of green light, a spinning wheel appeared.

*Oh,* Maddie thought. *That's not so bad.*

"What is that? I've never seen one before." Princess Aurora stepped forward and reached out her hand. She seemed strangely drawn to the spindle.

"No!" the others all cried. Everyone leaped forward to block her.

As they collided, Maddie stumbled into the spinning wheel. She felt a sharp prick on her finger.

Maddie raised her hand. A single drop of blood welled on her fingertip. She looked from her finger to the horrified faces of her friends.

Then everything went black.

CHAPTER
NINE

In her dream, Maddie was riding Samson around the ring. But this time they weren't at Sunny Stables. They were in Horsetail Hollow. Samson was galloping round and round the wishing well!

And they weren't alone. *Maximus* was galloping alongside them! On his back was a girl Maddie had never seen before.

Maddie looked to her other side. Angus and

Philippe were there, too. They were carrying riders, a boy and girl about Maddie's age. The kids' faces were alight with joy. The horses were running free, and there was magic in the air.

In that moment, Maddie knew the right wish.

*Not* my *wish*, she thought. Our *wish* . . .

Fuzzy lips nuzzled Maddie's cheek. Maddie's eyelids fluttered open.

The first thing she saw was a great, big horse's nose—right in her face!

"She's awake!" someone said. "Step back. Give her air."

The nose disappeared. Maddie saw Mom and Dad looking down at her. Their faces were full of concern.

What had happened? All Maddie remembered was a prick on her finger, a flash of green light, Maleficent laughing—

What were Mom and Dad doing in Maleficent's castle?

Maddie tried to sit up, but her head swam. "Take it easy," Mom said, helping her lie down again. "Don't try to rush. You've been out for a long time."

Maddie saw a swallow's nest high above in the

rafters. She felt scratchy straw beneath her. This was no castle. It was the barn! She was back in Horsetail Hollow!

Maddie rubbed her head. "I had the wildest dream. I dreamed I was in Maleficent's castle. There were goblins. And a spinning wheel—"

"You've been asleep for hours," Dad said. "You really had us worried, kiddo."

"We tried and tried to wake you. But nothing worked," Mom added. "And then Evie thought of Samson."

*Samson?*

This time, Maddie sat right up.

Samson was there in the barn! Macy and Evie stood with him, resting their hands on his neck.

But they weren't the only ones. Briar Rose and Prince Phillip were there, too! They stood to one side, holding hands. And the three good fairies were with them, wide-awake and smiling.

Even Rosalyn was there. Macy's grandmother stood near the door, watching the whole scene with her dark, twinkling eyes.

"I knew the only thing that could wake you up from Maleficent's curse was true love's kiss," Evie explained to Maddie. "A kiss from Samson! Because no one loves horses more than you."

"And horses love you, too," Macy added.

Maddie looked around at the smiling faces. She couldn't believe they were all together. "So it *wasn't* a dream."

"No," said Dad. "Believe it or not, this is really happening." He looked as if he could hardly believe it himself.

"But how did you escape from the castle?" Maddie asked Macy and Evie.

"When you got cursed instead of Aurora, Maleficent was so mad. She turned herself into a fire-breathing dragon!" Macy explained. "Prince Phillip had to slay her. It was epic!"

"It's all thanks to Evie and Macy," Prince Phillip said. "They gave me enchanted weapons. I lost the sword in the battle. But I still have this."

Phillip held up a charred shield. Beneath the burn marks, Maddie could make out the faint image of a cupcake.

"I'm sorry I missed it," said Maddie. But she wasn't really. A battle with a dragon seemed like a good thing to sleep through.

Maddie suddenly remembered her dream. She turned to her parents. "Mom, Dad, you can't sell the land. We need the wishing well!"

Her parents looked surprised. "How did you know about that?" Dad asked.

"It doesn't matter now," Maddie said. "The important thing is that Horsetail Hollow has a special destiny. I saw it in my dream. This is no ordinary farm—it's magical! You see it now, right? The well has been trying to show us all along! It should be a place where kids can learn how to ride and care for and love horses. And they'll learn from the very best teachers."

Maddie got up and went to Samson. She petted him, and he nuzzled her hair.

"A fairy-tale horse has to be loyal, brave, patient,

and kind. They have to have a big heart, and they love adventure," Maddie explained.

Samson nickered modestly. *Who, me?*

"There's no horse more special than a fairy-tale horse," Maddie went on. "That's why they're perfect for a magical riding stable!"

"Yes!" exclaimed Macy.

"Eee!" squealed Evie, clapping her hands.

But Mom and Dad didn't look so sure.

"I can't deny Horsetail Hollow is magical," Mom said, glancing around at all their new friends. "But a *riding stable*, Maddie? We don't know anything about taking care of horses."

"I can help you with that," Rosalyn spoke up. "Caring for horses is what I do best. I always thought there was something special about Horsetail Hollow. I just didn't know what it was. I guess it just took the right person to come along and see it," she added, giving Maddie a wink.

Dad cleared his throat. "We still have one problem. How will we pay for it? We'd need to fix up the barn and the rest of the farm, and we're barely getting by as it is."

Prince Phillip stepped forward. "I'll gladly help with that," he said. "After all, you girls saved my life . . . and our kingdom." He squeezed Aurora's hand, and she smiled back at him.

Dad looked flabbergasted. "That's . . . very generous!"

"It would be my honor. Our name—Phillip— means 'friend to horses,' after all," the prince said with a smile.

"Thank you, Prince Phillip!" Maddie could hardly contain her excitement. Her dream was going to come true!

"I have one more favor to ask." She turned to the three good fairies. "Whenever our horse friends come to Horsetail Hollow, things go wrong in their fairy-tale worlds. Can you help us so they can visit without causing any problems?"

"I think we can manage that," said Flora.

"Here is a gift for you, Maddie." Merryweather twirled her wand in the air. A tiny silver horseshoe on a chain appeared. The fairy hung the necklace around Maddie's neck.

"Whenever you need our help, you can call us with this charm," she said. "Just ask, and we'll appear."

Maddie studied the charm. It held tiny gems of red, green, and blue. "I'll take good care of it," she promised.

"And now it's time for us to go home," Flora said. "I know King Stefan and everyone else in the castle are eager to see the princess."

Everyone went to the well to see them off. Mom, Dad, and Rosalyn shook hands with Princess Aurora, Prince Phillip, and the fairies. Maddie,

Macy, and Evie gave Samson extra hugs. But for once, Maddie wasn't sad to say good-bye. She knew she would see him again soon.

Princess Aurora kissed each girl's cheek. "I'll miss you," she told them. "But I'll come back and visit. Being a princess isn't as bad as I thought. Some things haven't changed."

The princess gave them a secret smile. Then she lifted the hem of her gown. Beneath the long, elegant dress, she was barefoot.

Prince Phillip produced two coins from his pocket. He handed one to Maddie. Then the prince, Aurora, and the fairies put out their hands. Samson added his hoof. They made their wish. *Whoosh!* They were gone.

Now it was Maddie's turn. "We need everyone's hands. For this wish to come true, we all need to want it *together.*"

It was just like she'd told Briar Rose: Why make

a wish for just yourself, when your wish could make everyone happy?

Evie put her hand on Maddie's. Macy put her hand on Evie's. Rosalyn added hers, too.

"Well?" Maddie said to her parents. "Are you in?"

Dad looked at Mom. Mom looked at Dad. Then they both started to laugh.

"Why not?" Dad said.

"Why not?" Mom agreed. "A magical horse farm. Who would have imagined?"

They placed their hands in, too.

Maddie closed her eyes. She spoke aloud the wish that filled her heart.

"We wish for Horsetail Hollow to be a safe place for magical horses and the riders who love them."

The wind didn't blow this time. The world didn't spin. But something *was* happening.

They saw a shimmering light. It spread outward

from the well, touching everything like frost. It glazed the tall grass and flowers and each leaf on the trees. It crept up the barn walls, over the roof, all the way to the horse-shaped weather vane. It touched the garden, the farmhouse, and even the chicken coop, until everything was bathed in silvery light.

The light flared for a brief instant, then it died away. But Maddie could tell from the tingling of her skin that the magic was still there. It was all around them.

"Well," Dad said after a long moment. "This has been quite a day."

"I'll say," said Rosalyn. "How's that for a happy ending?"

"No," said Maddie.

Everyone looked at her.

"No?" Mom asked.

"Nope." Maddie grinned. "This is just the beginning."

# All-New Illustrated Chapter Books Inspired by Disney Classic Movies